Delmar the Dinky

Written by **Pat Danna**

Illustrated by **Pardeep Mehra**

Pat Danna

In memory of Harold Noss, who inspired me to write
this story after listening to his hilarious tales of riding
the Brentwood dinky as a child in St. Louis.

Illustrations by Pardeep Mehra
Cover & Layout by Praise Saflor

Publisher's Cataloging-in-Publication data

Names: Danna, Pat, author. | Mehra, Pardeep, illustrator.
Title: Delmar the Dinky / Pat Danna ; illustrated by Pardeep Mehra.
Description: St. Louis, MO: Pat Danna, 2021. | Summary: Delmar the Dinky is a small
trolley who is always pushed to the back of the rail yard; but when the 1904 World's Fair
comes to St. Louis, he will have his chance to prove he can carry passengers to the fair.
Identifiers: LCCN: 2020920713 | 978-1-7359960-2-8 (hardcover) |
978-1-7359960-0-4 (paperback) | 978-1-7359960-1-1 (ebook)
Subjects: LCSH Trolley cars--Juvenile fiction. | Trains--Juvenile fiction. | Louisiana Purchase
Exposition (1904 : Saint Louis, Mo.)--Juvenile fiction. | CYAC Trolley cars--Fiction. | Trains-
-Fiction. | Louisiana Purchase Exposition (1904 : Saint Louis, Mo.)--Fiction. | BISAC
JUVENILE FICTION /Transportation / Railroads & Trains | JUVENILE FICTION /
Transportation / General | JUVENILE FICTION / Historical / United States / 20th Century
Classification: LCC PZ7.1.D313 Del 2021 | DDC [E]--dc23

What is a dinky?

A small streetcar, called a *dinky*, carried as many as 40 passengers on the same rail lines that were used by trains and larger streetcars. The dinky ran on electric power connected to overhead wires with a trolley pole. In St. Louis, the Loop Trolley may one day travel down Delmar Boulevard to Forest Park. Who knows? Maybe someday you will ride a dinky.

With permission of the Brentwood, Missouri, Historical Society.

"Yoo hoo! I'm over here!" shouted Delmar to a crowd gathered at the train station on a hot summer day. Everyone was going to the World's Fair and needed a trolley to take them there.

Delmar was a small trolley called a *dinky*.

"Yoo hoo! Over here!" Delmar shouted again.
"I may be the smallest trolley in the rail yard, but I can
do something that no other trolley can do."

But today Delmar parked behind the trains and big trolleys, all the way in the back of the rail yard.

"I can take people to the World's Fair," Delmar said sadly, "but I'm stuck back here."

People stand in line and wait...and wait.

"Where is the dinky?" they asked.

"Here I am, over here," he yelled.

No one heard Delmar over
the noise of the rail yard.

"See my shiny headlight?"
No one saw his headlight flash.

"See my yellow color?"
No one noticed his bright paint.

"My wicker seats are comfortable."
No one looked his way.

"I only charge five cents for a ride!" he cried out.

Still, no one heard him.

Delmar had an idea. "I need to get Conductor Noss' attention."

Delmar squeezed between two trolleys and nudged his way closer to the station.

He rang his bell.

DING!
DING!
DING!

He flicked his headlight.

"I'll rev my engine," said Delmar.
"Maybe now Conductor Noss will notice me."

Suddenly…

"Look! The dinky!"
said Conductor Noss.
"There you are!
We need your help to take
people to the fair."

He grabbed his cap and jumped aboard Delmar.

"Me? Yay! He finally picked ME!" Delmar shouted as loud as he could.

The switchman
waved his lantern.

The conductor hit the throttle.

"All aboard! Watch your step!" announced Conductor Noss.

Delmar rattled and swayed down the track.

"HOORAY!" cheered the passengers.

"Uh-oh...traffic jam," said Delmar as he came
to two big trolleys slowly rumbling along.
But Delmar could do something the
other trolleys couldn't do.

Delmar took a deep breath. He looked to the left, then to the right, and quickly switched to the inside track.

He scooted between
the two big trolleys!

CLICKETY
CLACK!

CLICKETY
CLACK!

CLICKETY
CLACK!

Delmar pulled into the station, right on time.

"I may be small," he said, "but I'm the best trolley of all."

Made in the USA
Monee, IL
23 May 2021